# SCHULTHEISS

# BELL'S THEOREM

catalan communications
new york

BELL'S THEOREM
Story and illustration by Matthias Schultheiss
Translation by Tom Leighton
Edited by Bernd Metz

Published by Catalan Communications
43 East 19th Street
New York, NY 10003

AN ALBIN MICHEL BOOK

ISBN 0-87416-037-5
Dep. L.B. 4903-87

First Printing February 1987
Printed in Catalonia (Spain)
ALVAGRAF, S.A. C/. Gerona, 6 - La Llagosta (Barcelona)

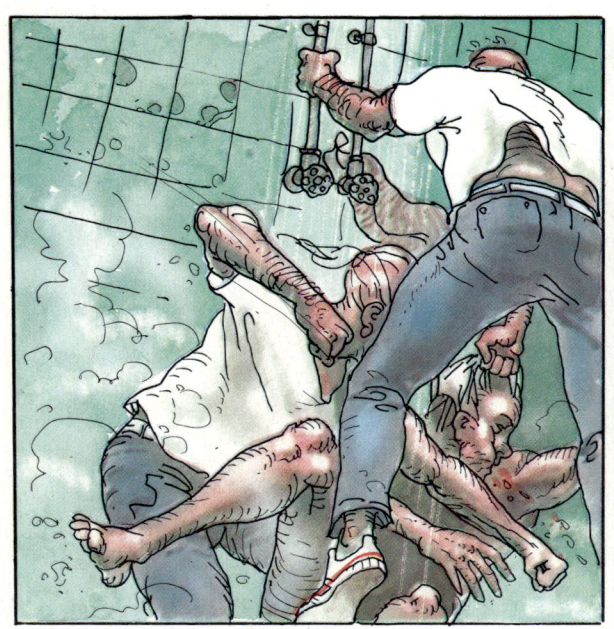

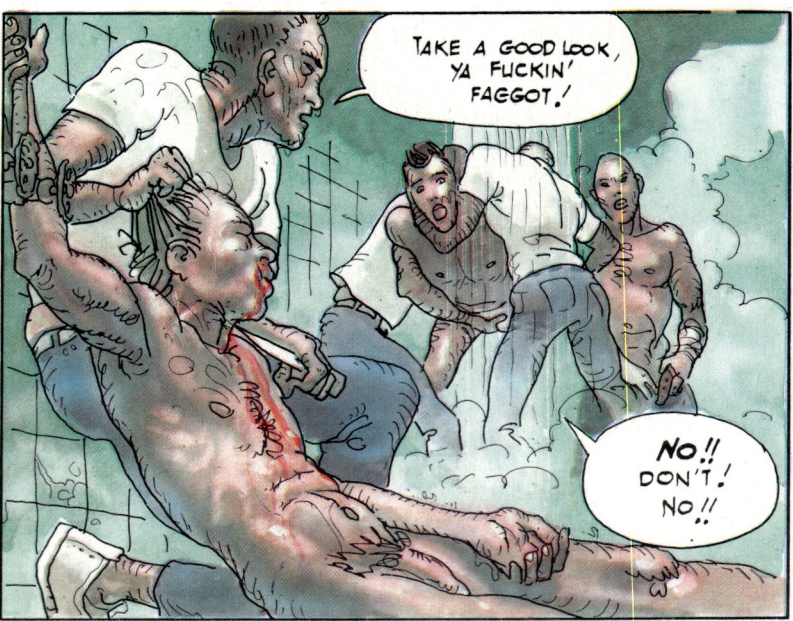

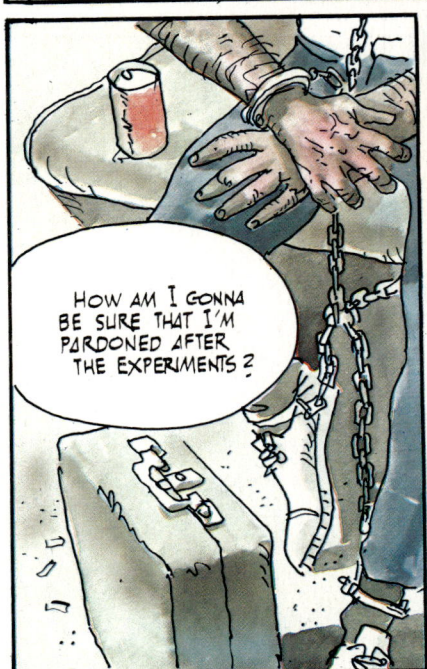

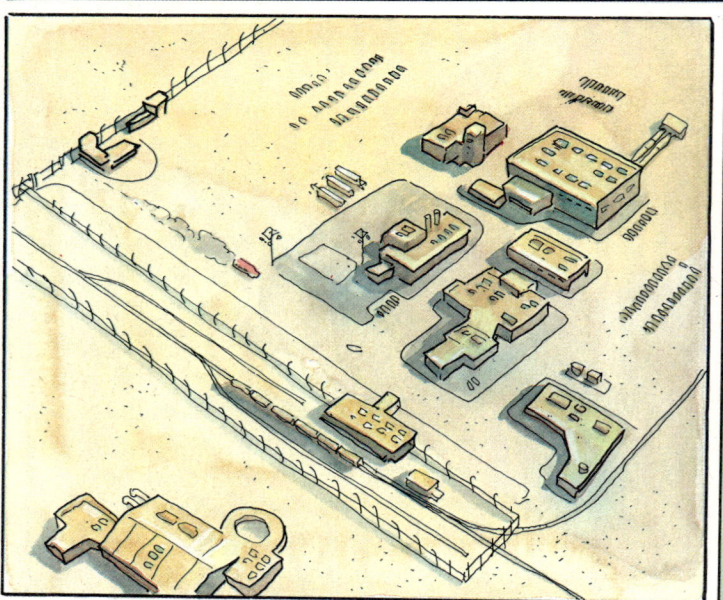

SHALBY. HE'S
EXPECTED. HERE
ARE HIS
TRANSFER PAPERS,
ALL SIGNED.

SHALBY, AGE 38,
CAUCASIAN, LIFER...
O.K., LEE, TAKE
THE CHAINS
OFF!

WAIT HERE. DON'T GET
THE IDEA WE'RE SERVING
CHAMPAGNE AND CAVIAR
AROUND HERE! AND DON'T
PULL ANYTHING, THE DOC
WANTS GUYS IN GOOD
SHAPE.

YEAH...

6

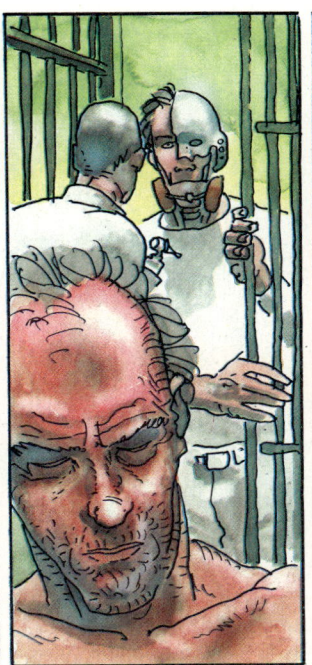

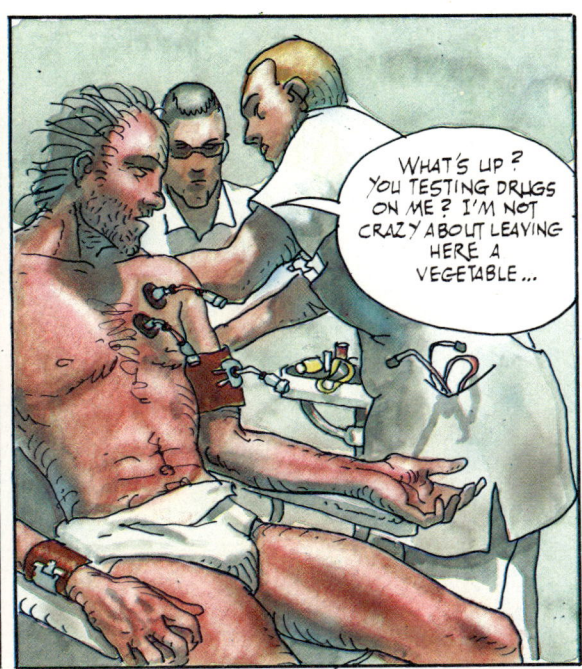

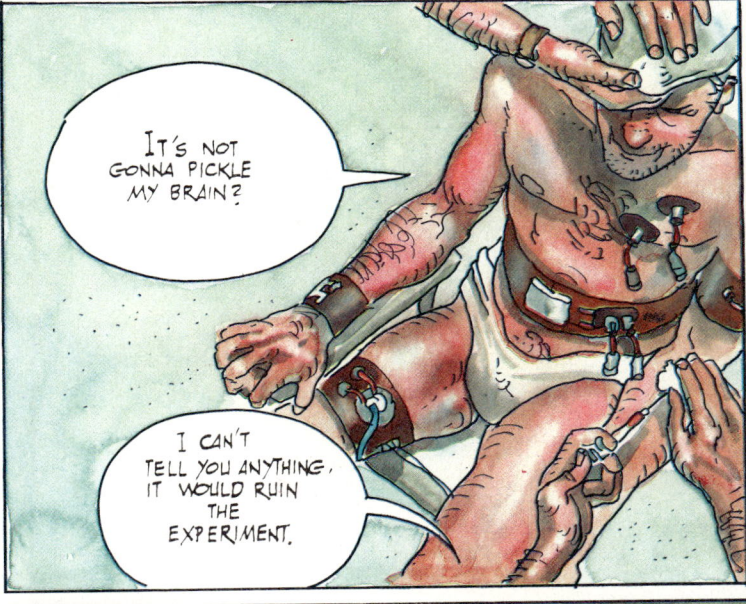

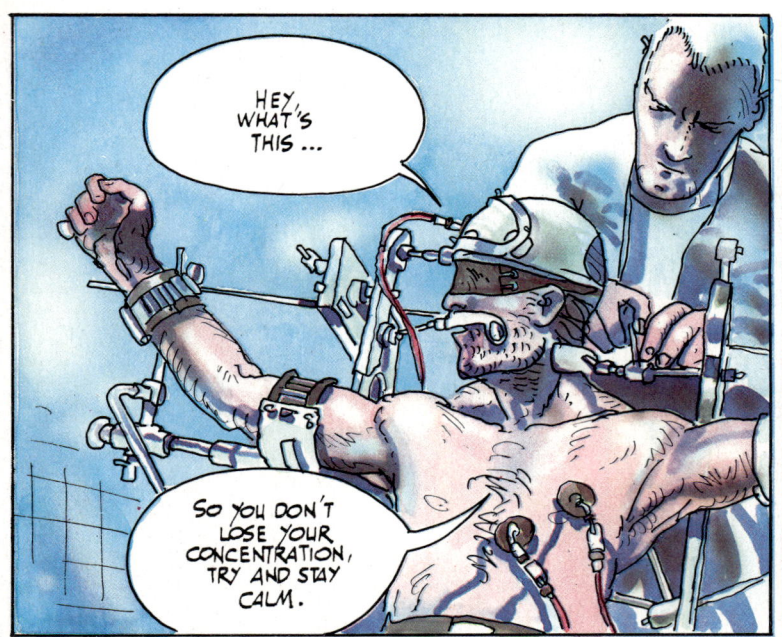
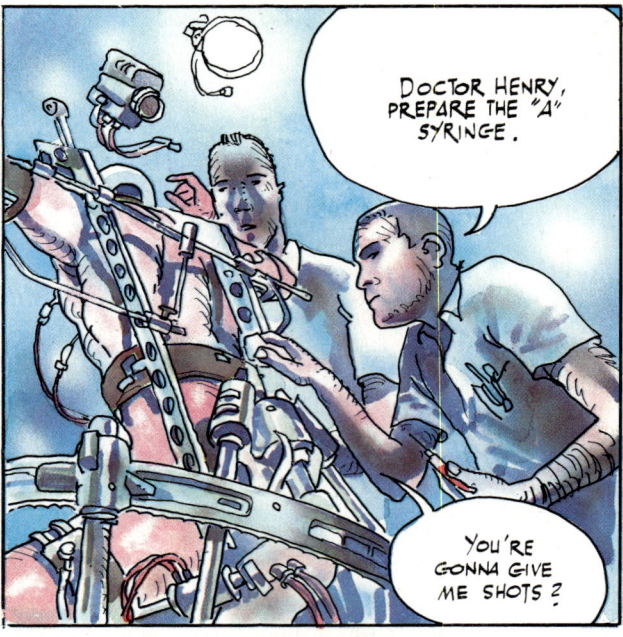
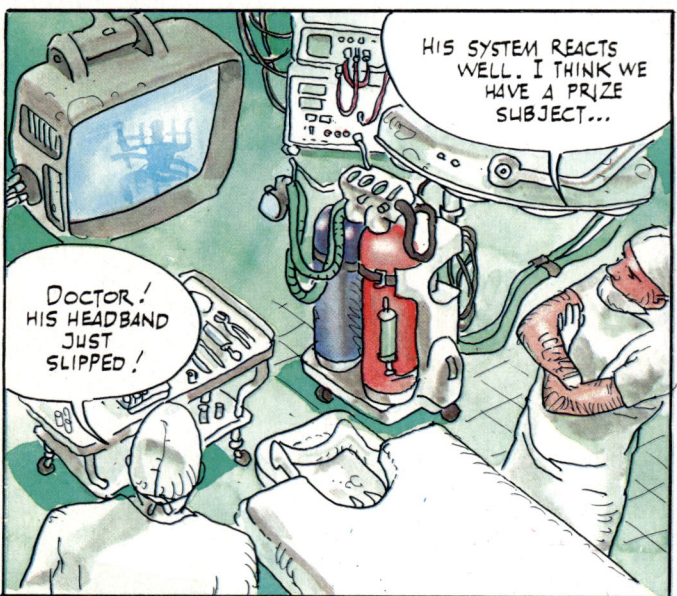
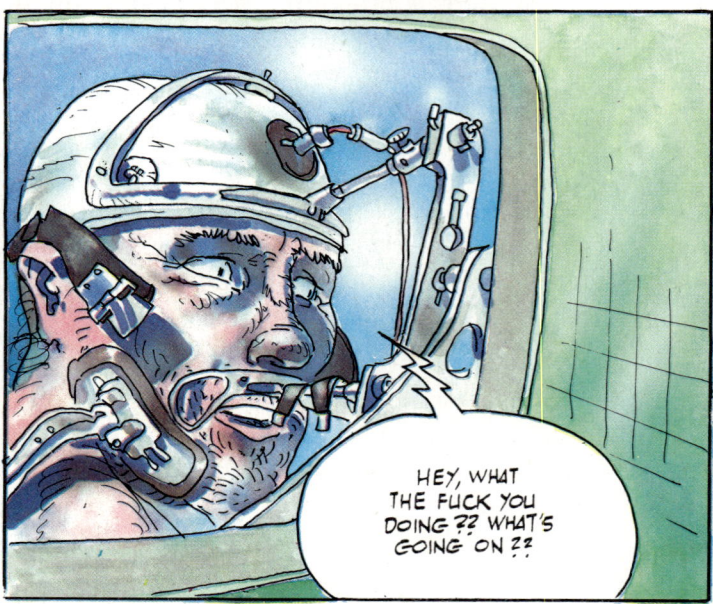
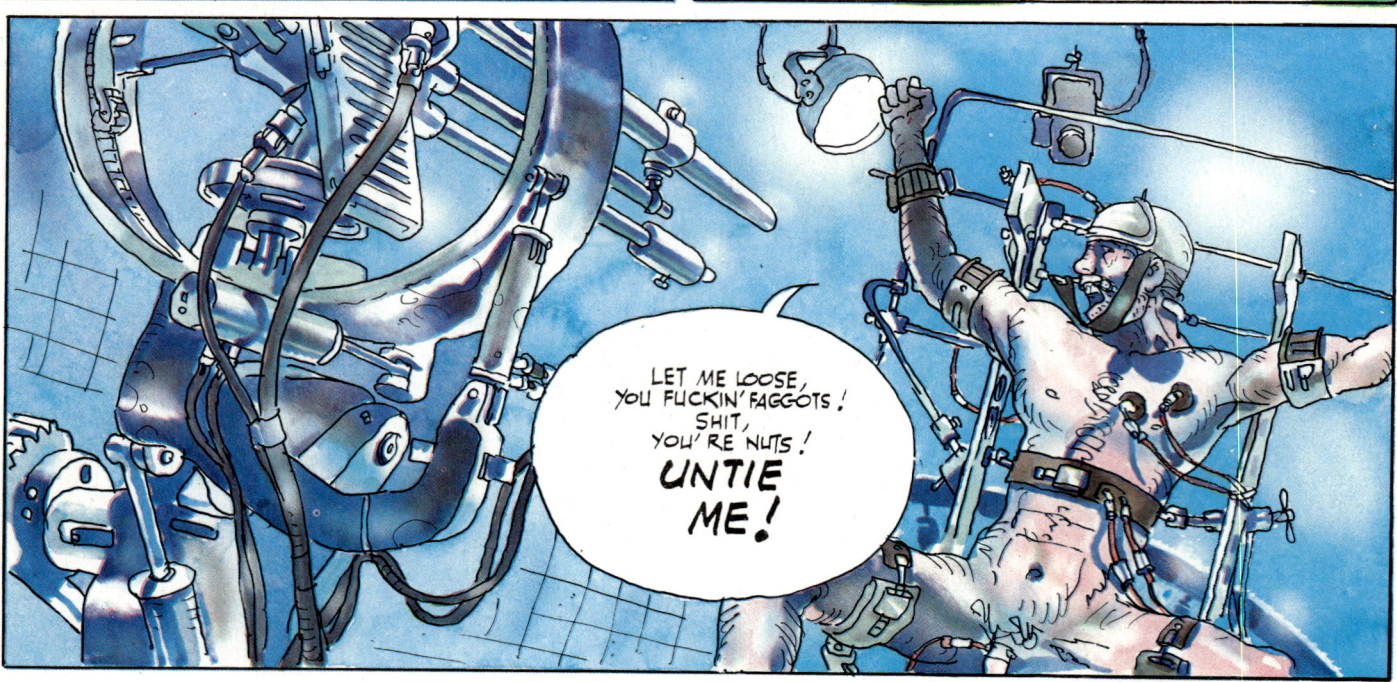

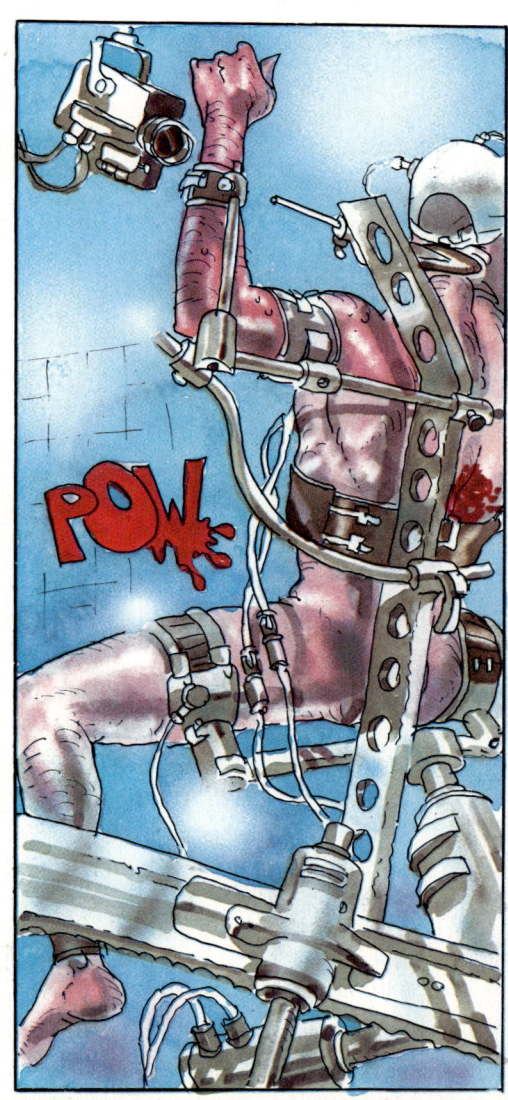

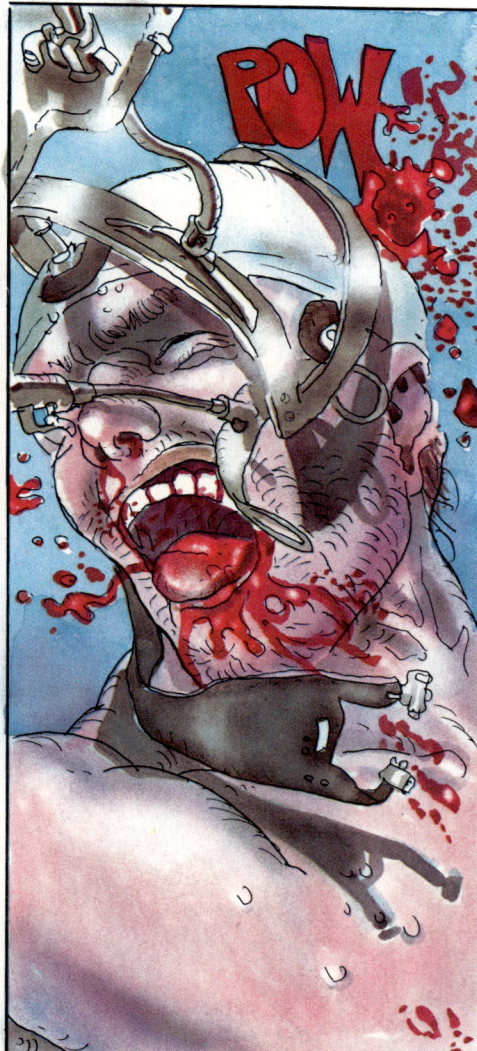

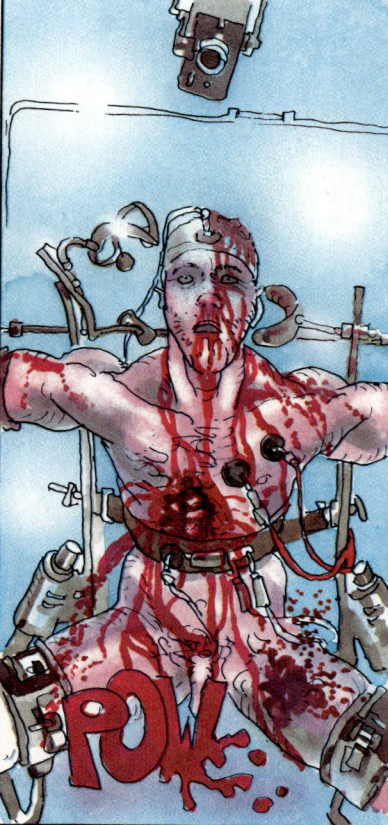

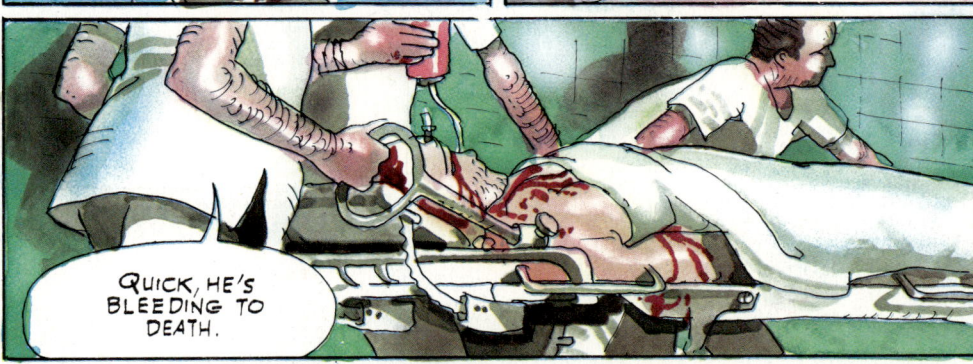

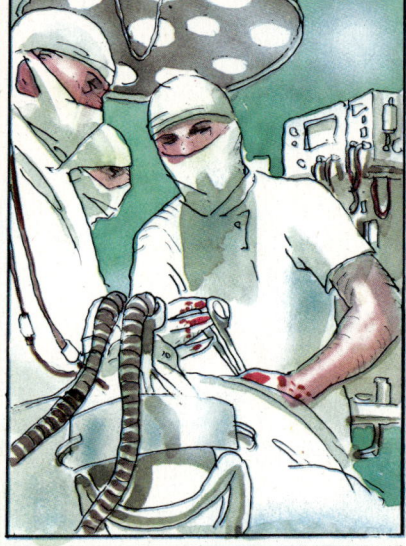

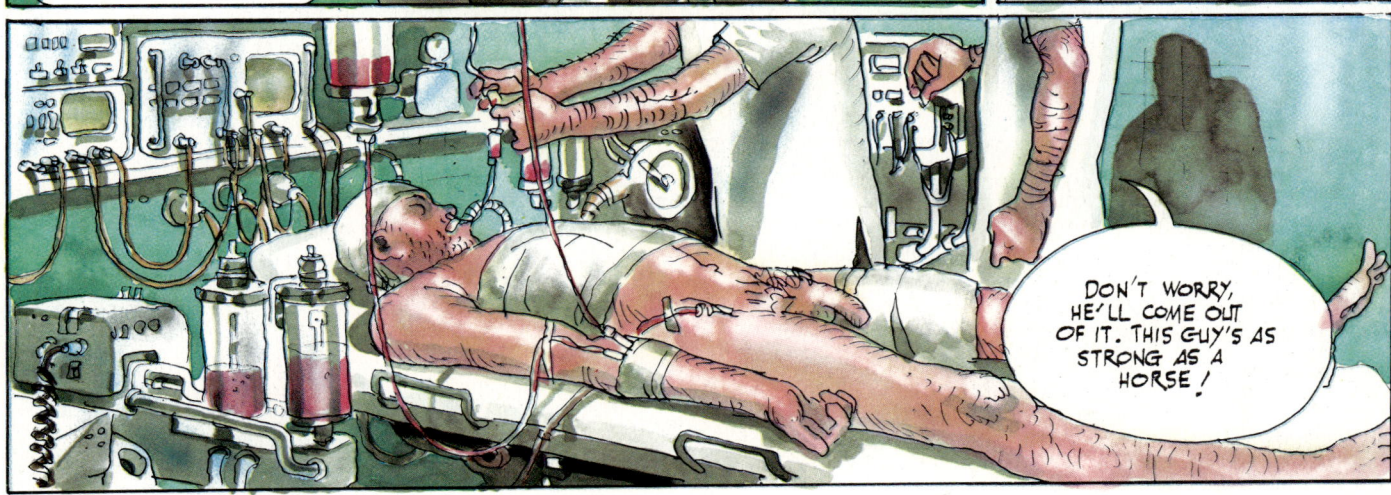

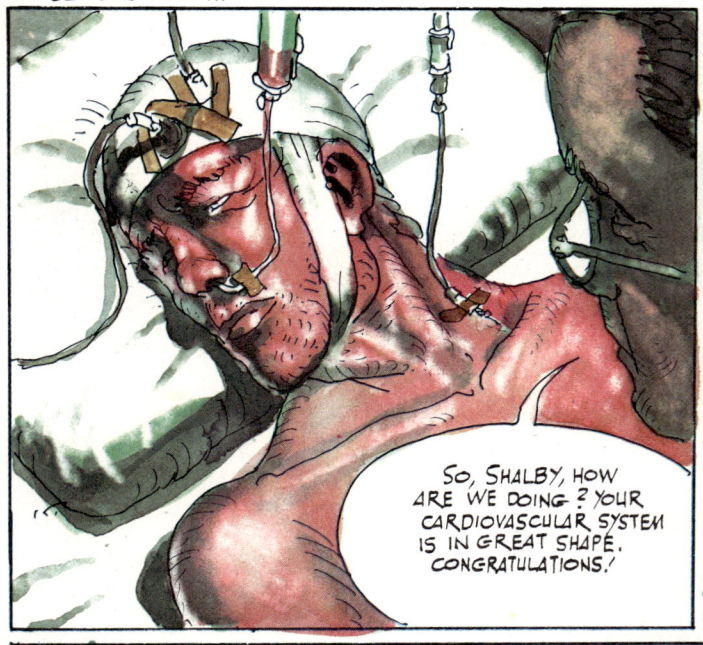

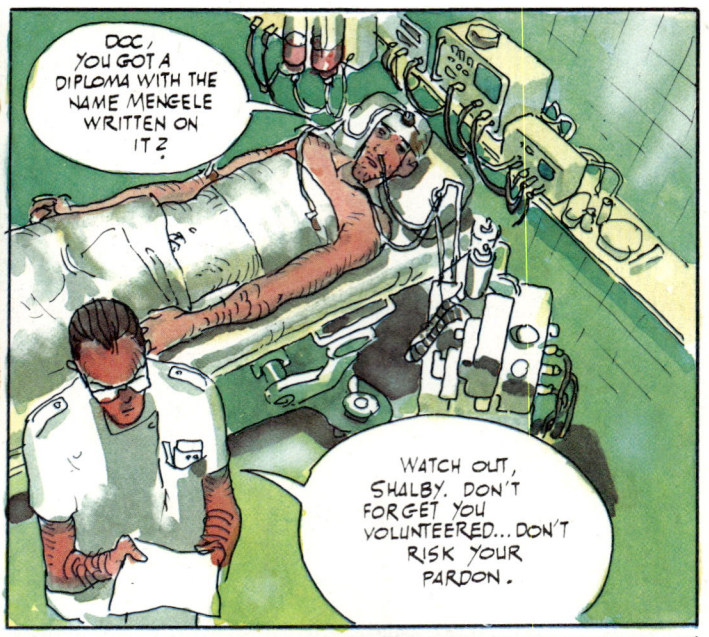

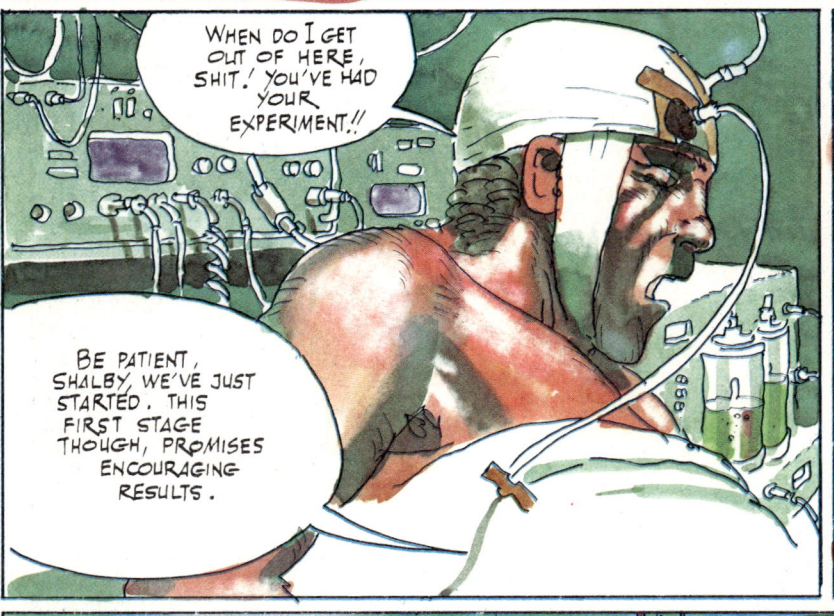

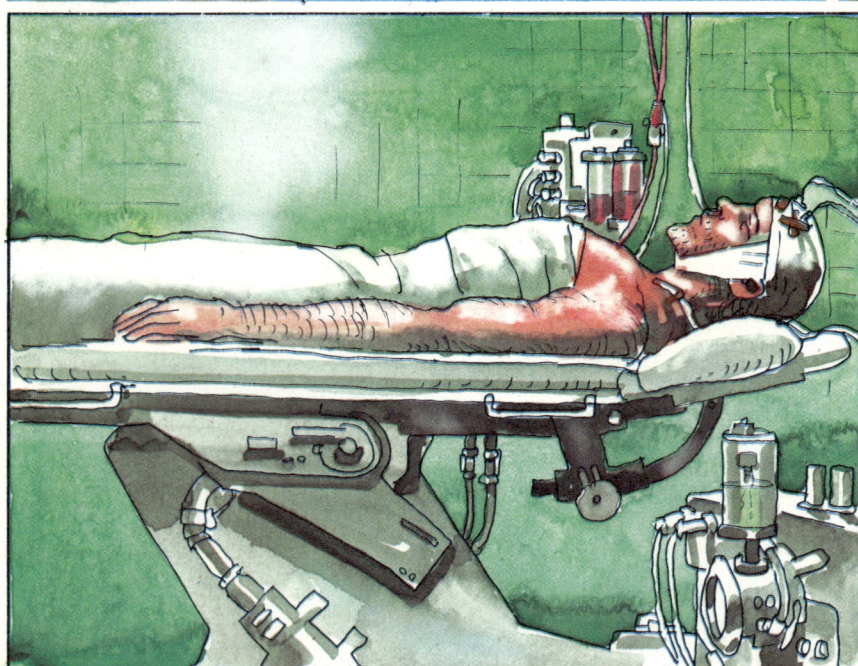

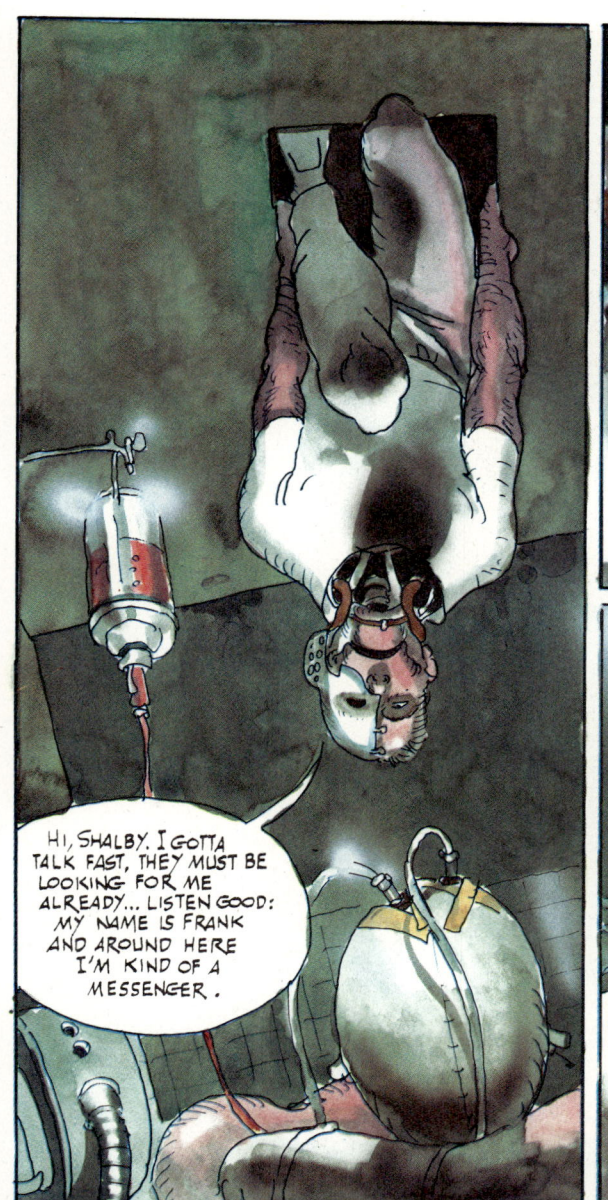

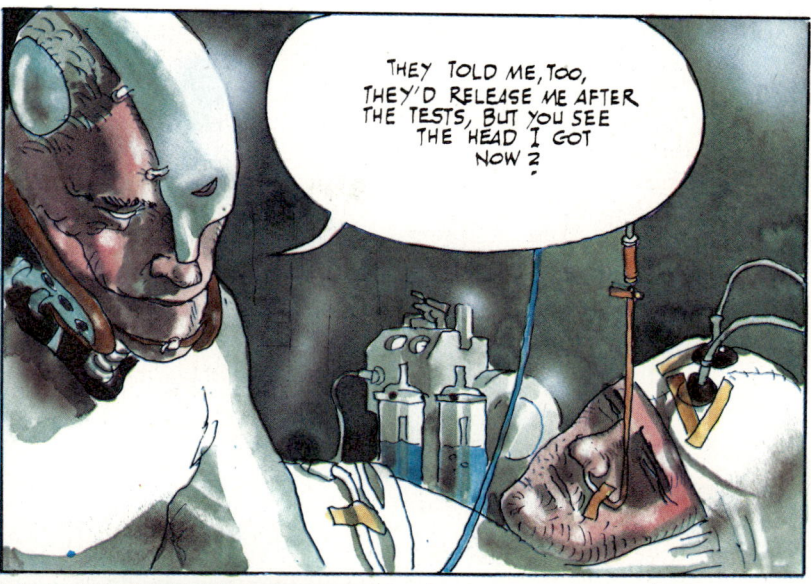

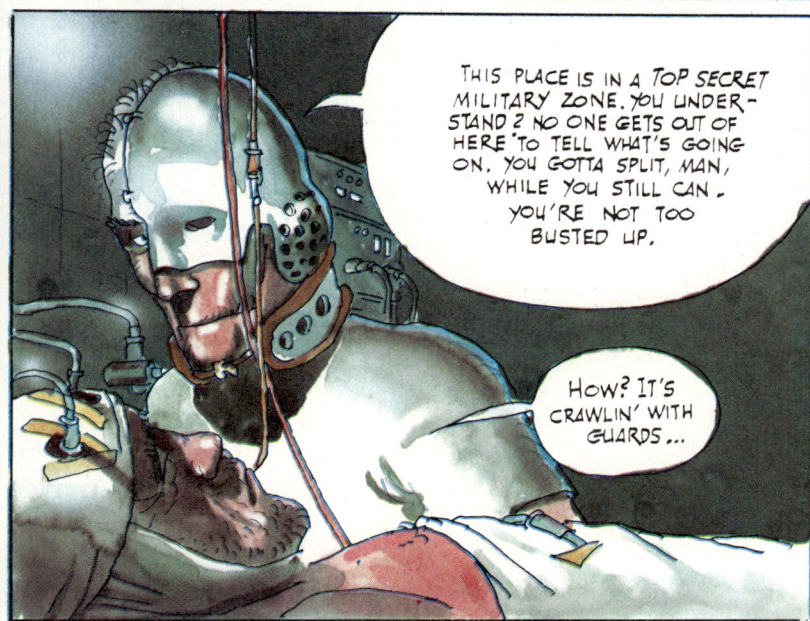

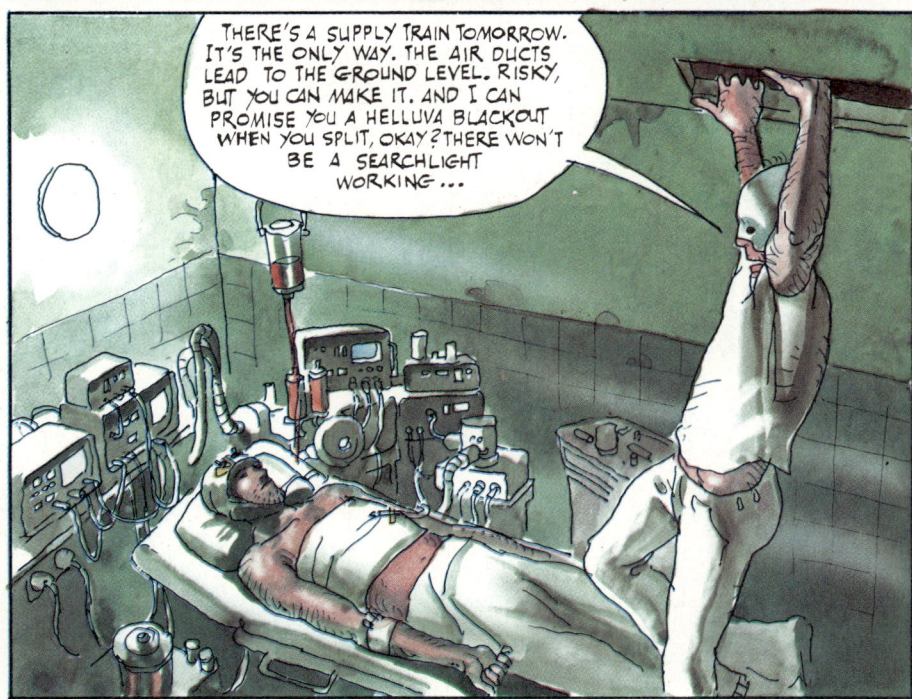

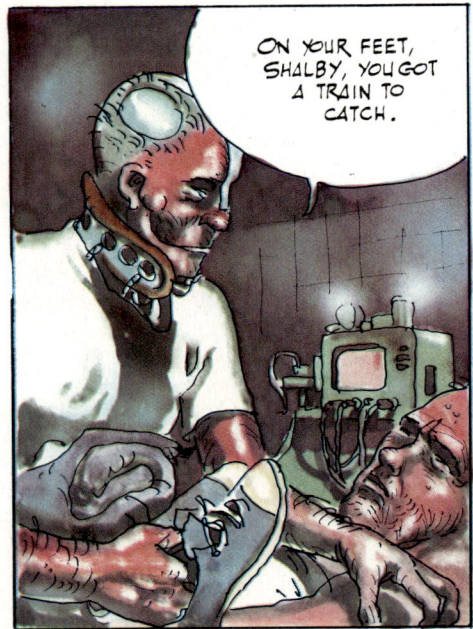

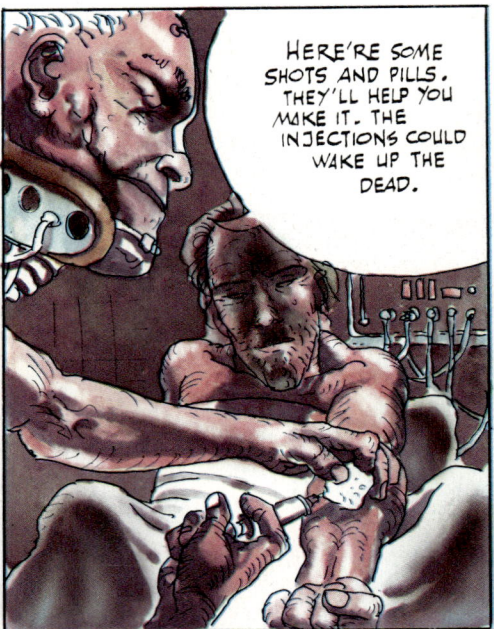

14

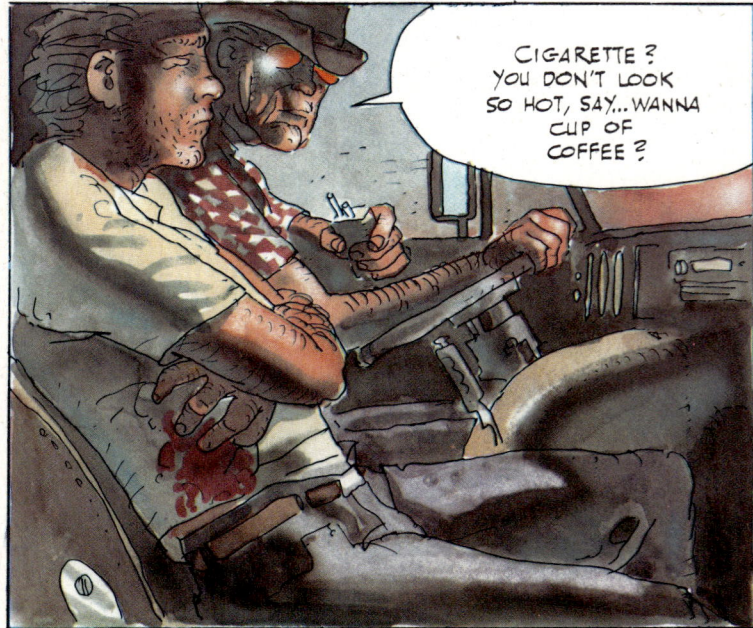

16

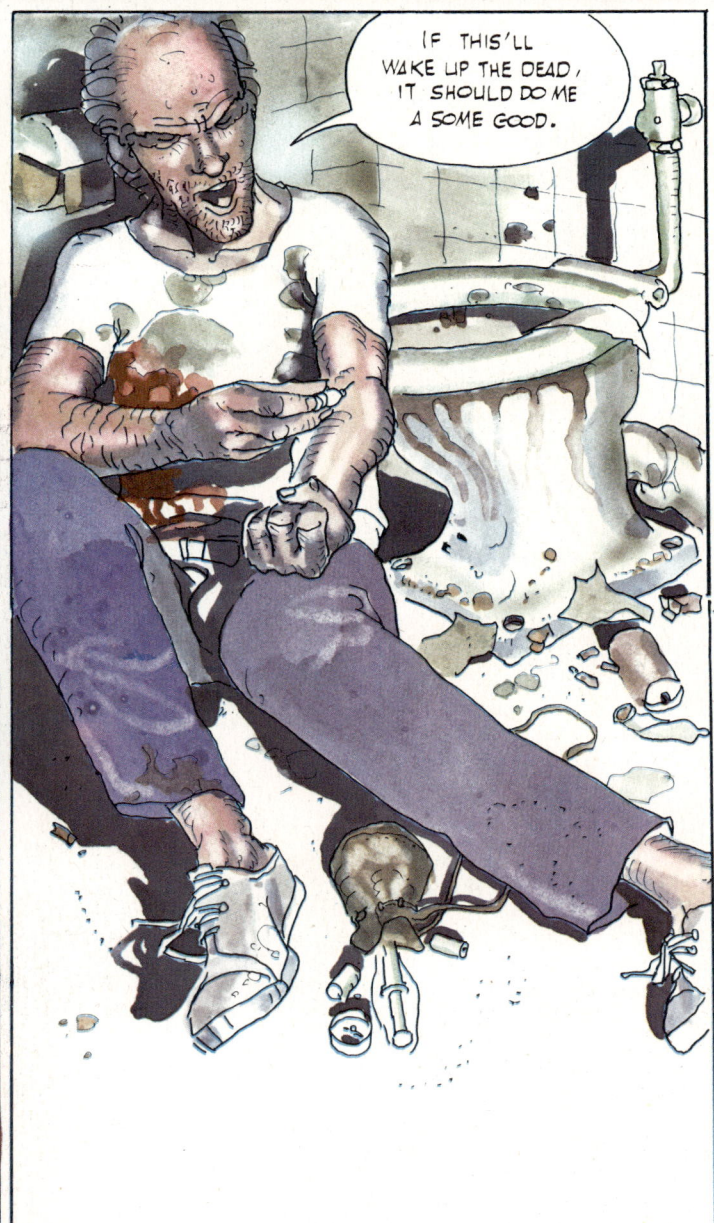

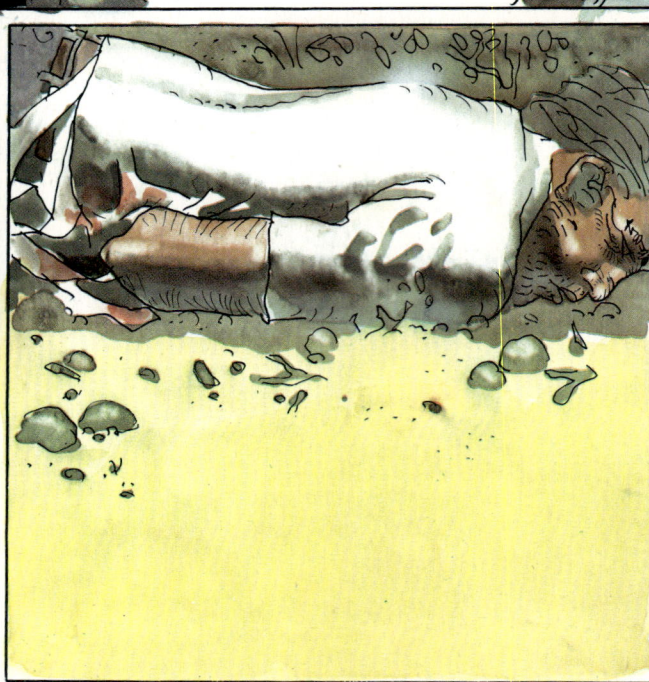

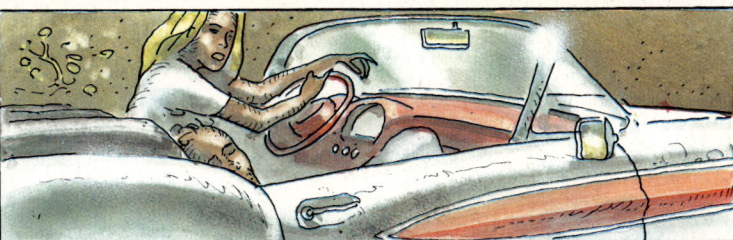

21

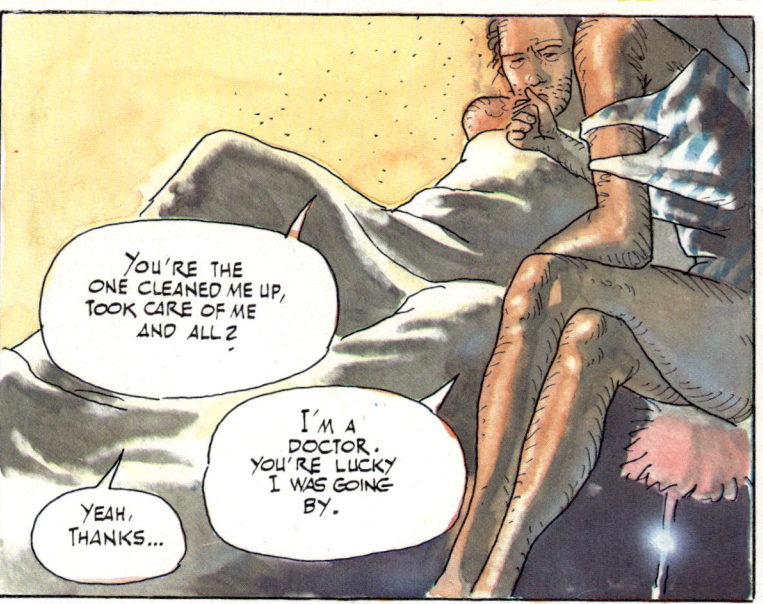

22

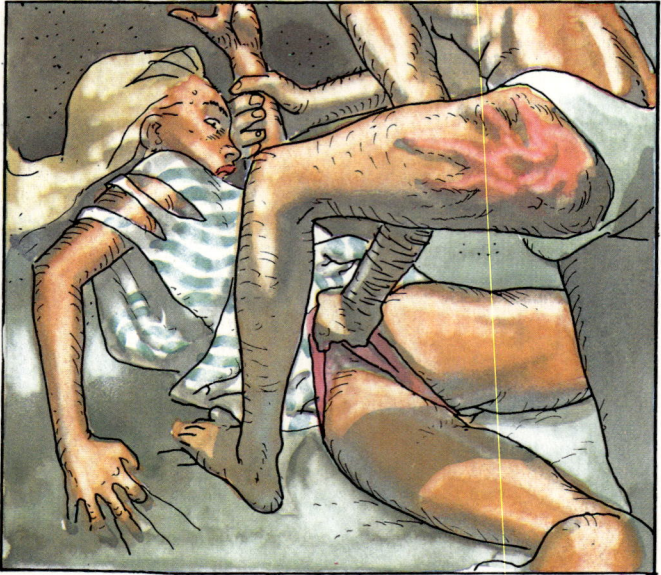

26

MARK AMSELTEIN, PHYSICIST FROM HAMBURG, GERMANY... AND A THOUSAND BUCKS, HA, HA.

FUCK, IT'S ME! EXACTLY THE SAME MUG!

WHAT'S THIS? HIS DIARY... LET'S HAVE A LOOK: "3-4-78: THERE EXIST CONCRETE SITUATIONS, INTERDEPENDENT, ALTHOUGH SEPARATED IN TIME AND SPACE. HAD TO INTERRUPT THE EXPERIMENT, CONVINCED OF INFLUENCING ANOTHER EXISTENCE, TERRIBLE PAINS."

THAT DOESN'T SHED MUCH LIGHT... HMM... I'D BETTER BURY YOU, MAN, BUT LIKE I GET THE IDEA YOU'D RATHER STAY ON THE PHONE. THE NEWS IS GOOD, ANYWAY?

EVERY TIME THE WHALES COME BACK, THE HEADPHONES START CRACKLING.

IT'S TOO COMPLICATED FOR ME. I'M GOING OUT FOR SOME AIR.

GOTTA GET OUT OF HERE. I GOT ONE CHANCE LEFT: I TAKE THE GUY'S PAPERS, HIS DOUGH, AND GO SET UP IN GERMANY, BEFORE THOSE FAGGOTS GET ME.

HIS DIARY AND HIS SKETCHES, TOO. I'M GONNA HAVE TO KNOW HIS STORY TO REPLACE HIM.

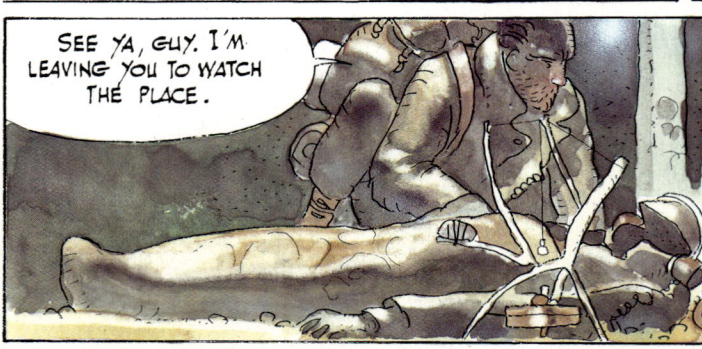

SEE YA, GUY. I'M LEAVING YOU TO WATCH THE PLACE.

NO MAP, JUST A COMPASS, SHALBY HAS TO MOVE FAST: WINTER IS NEAR, AND WITH IT, SNOW!

DOWN THERE! FOOTPRINTS!

THE TEMPERATURE DROPS VERY QUICKLY. THE FIRST SNOWSTORMS HIT, SILENT AND THREATENING.

GAME HAS DISAPPEARED. THE COLD IS HORRIBLE.

HE DOESN'T DARE TO SLEEP, AFRAID HE WON'T WAKE UP AGAIN. ONE DAY HE MANAGES TO HUNT DOWN A SQUIRREL.

BUT SHALBY PUSHES ON. HE KNOWS THAT HE WON'T BE BROUGHT DOWN BY HUNGER OR COLD...

You trappers are a funny bunch. You live for years like savages and all at once, in one night, you junk it all.

Yeah, yeah.

It's Mark Amseltein who buys a ticket: Montreal to Hamburg via Amsterdam.

There. Now Shalby no longer exists!

A JACK DANIELS, PLEASE. NO ICE.

YOU ALONE? LET ME BUY YOU A DRINK.

WHY? IS IT YOUR BIRTHDAY?

YES... IT'S THE FIRST YEAR OF MY NEW LIFE!

OH, JEEZUS! I WAS EXPECTING WORSE... YOU'RE A LUCKY GUY, I STILL GOTTA WRESTLE WITH MY OLD SKIN.

IT DOESN'T LOOK OLD TO ME.

HUM. SO LET'S HAVE A DRINK TO THIS NEW LIFE OF YOURS! WHAT ARE YOU GOING TO DO WITH IT?

TO TELL THE TRUTH, I DON'T KNOW, EXCEPT NO MATTER WHAT... TRY NOT TO MAKE THE SAME MISTAKES ALL OVER AGAIN.

GEE! I'D FEEL LOST WITHOUT MY "MISTAKES".

45

POP
TCOCK
TCOOK
TCOCK
LAST CALL FOR PASSENGERS FOR AIR CANADA FLIGHT 2014 QUEBEC - MONTREAL - AMSTERDAM - HAMBURG. BOARDING IMMEDIATELY.
YOU'RE GONNA MEET UP WITH MAGOON. SEE YOU IN HELL, FUCKER.

SHALBY ISN'T THE SAME ANYMORE. SCHIZOPHRENIA? OR JUST THE RESULT OF ALL HE'S BEEN THROUGH? IT DOESN'T MATTER. EVEN IF HE WANTED TO, HE COULDN'T CHANGE WHAT'S GOING TO HAPPEN NEXT.